The Kitten Who Wants To Fall Asleep

A Story To Help Children Go To Sleep

Cecilia Egan

National Library of Australia Cataloguing-in-Publication entry

Creator: Egan, Cecilia - author.

Title: The kitten who wants to fall asleep : a story to help children go to sleep / Cecilia Egan ;
Elizabeth Alger, illustrator.

ISBN: 9781925110845 (paperback)

Target Audience: For pre-school age.

Subjects: Kittens--Juvenile fiction.
Sleep--Juvenile fiction.
Stories in rhyme.

Dewey Number: A823.3

ABN 67 099 575 078
PO Box 9113, Brighton, 3186, Victoria, Australia
www.leavesofgoldpress.com

To adults: How to read the story

Psychologists use a range of well-known and proven strategies to help people (of all ages) fall asleep. These methods have been woven into this bedtime tale.

The story is intended to be read aloud by an older person when it is time for the child to go to sleep, and preferably when the child is already lying in bed. Children can look at the pictures if they wish, but the methods are most effective if they are simply listening. One of the sleep-promoting tactics used in this book is 'visualization', and when children are not looking at the pictures they are visualizing their own pictures.

They can, by all means, look at the pictures at other times.

Before you start, make sure the child is snug in bed; not too hot and not too cold, and lying down in a comfortable position.

Try to make the bedroom QUIET, DARK AND COOL. These three elements are important for good sleep.

Set aside a time for reading this bedtime story when you know you won't be interrupted by other people, phone calls etc. Interruptions can disrupt the child's visualizations and break the flow of the story.

Do not rush when reading. Slowing down is one of the keys to falling asleep, and if you clearly show that you are calm and unhurried, the child will feel calm and unhurried too. Read in a calm, slow, gentle voice.

As you read through the story you will sometimes be prompted to act out a performance or gesture, e.g. [pretend to sprinkle petals].

Certain words are in CAPITALS or underlined. If anything is written in CAPITAL LETTERS, really accentuate it and give it importance as you read. If anything is underlined, say it very leisurely and soothingly.

There are also places in the story where the reader can insert the name of a child or more than one child; e.g. [name] The use of square placeholder brackets is standard practice with personalized stories.

In many cases the child will fall asleep before you come to the end of the story. If this happens, you should continue to read the book from cover to cover. The child has trusted you to read the whole story and if they feel that their going to sleep will make you betray that trust, they might try to stay awake. You might think that if they are asleep they don't know you have stopped before the end, but you cannot be sure! People can still hear sounds while they sleep, and can even learn new things while they sleep.

Earn the child's trust by finishing the story as promised. If a child feels they are being watched over by a trust-worthy, dependable adult, he or she will feel safe and secure enough to let go and fall asleep.

Hints to promote falling asleep easily:

During the day let children play outdoors as often as possible. Sunlight regulates our melatonin levels and thus promotes refreshing sleep.

Physical exercise is naturally tiring. It makes us fall asleep more easily and stay asleep.

Stick to a prescribed pre-sleep routine every evening. Children can be taught to associate certain behaviors with going to sleep; activities such as cleaning their teeth and having a bed-time story read aloud to them. These reassuring patterns can help them fall asleep more easily.

Happy reading!

Cecilia Egan

The Kitten Who Wants To Fall Asleep

As you listen to me reading this book, you will feel <u>very</u> relaxed and tired. You might want to yawn, [yawn] and close your eyes and sink down deeper into your bed. You might even want to fall asleep, very easily, before we get to the last page.

You can fall asleep <u>any time</u>. I will still go on reading this story whether you fall asleep easily now, or whether you fall asleep at the end, like everyone in the story.

Once there was a little kitten whose name was Misti. She loved to laugh and run around with her friends and play with toys. She liked eating delicious food and listening to happy music, and sometimes she would dance to the music. Do you like doing these things too, [name]?

Every night at bedtime Misti knew she should go to sleep, because she was very tired.

But sometimes it was hard to fall asleep because she kept having lots of thoughts.

One evening Misti lay in bed <u>yawning</u> [yawn], but with every breath she took, she kept remembering all the playing and jumping and skipping and laughing she had done that day; all the activities that had tired her out so much that she wanted to lie down and rest.

She thought of the nice things she could be doing outdoors on the swings and the slide and the see-saw. All that sliding down, and all that rocking and rocking on the see-saw could make her so weary that she would want to curl up in bed and fall asleep EASILY!

Misti was really tired, but with so many thoughts in her mind she couldn't fall asleep right now.

Luckily Misti had a fairy grandmother to help her fall asleep. Fairy Grandmother has many strong magic spells that have helped Misti go to sleep before.

Everyone has a fairy grandmother, including you, [name]. Your fairy grandmother watches over you all the time, even though you can't see her. If you ask her, she will help you <u>fall asleep</u>.

Misti was wishing she could easily fall asleep.
"I am very tired," said Misti yawning. [yawn] "I want to fall asleep, and so do you, [name]. Let's call my fairy grandmother to come here from Sleepyland. Fairy grandmother, can you help us fall asleep now?"

Misti's fairy grandmother appeared at the bedside, sleepily rubbing her eyes.

"Hello [name]," she said. "Hello Misti. I am glad you called me. I was just thinking about going to sleep now."

Fairy Grandmother had a kind face, and wings like a butterfly, and soft fur and a pretty dress. She was carrying a basket and a magic wand.

Two small, drowsy elves floated lazily in the air near her shoulders and three girl teddy bears in skirts sat yawning at her feet. The teddy bears were very little, and one was really tiny.

Fairy Grandmother waved her wand and suddenly Misti was snuggled up beside YOU in YOUR bed. Her fur felt soft and warm.

"I like snuggling up with you, [name], said Misti.

"This is a magic basket to keep your thoughts safe till tomorrow," said Fairy Grandmother. "If you put your thoughts inside, my helper elves will take them to the workshop in Sleepyland. The elves are good at finding answers to any problems you were thinking about. They will bring back your thoughts tomorrow morning and give them to you, all fresh, as soon as you wake up."

She opened the lid of the basket. "Now put your thoughts in here and you won't have to think of them till tomorrow morning."

[Make a 'basket' by cupping your hands together. Offer your hands to the child, who can pretend to put his or her thoughts inside. Then bring your hands slowly together to 'close the basket'. Pretend to give the thoughts to the invisible elves in the air.]

The elves took the magic basket and slowly flew off. They were almost TOO SLEEPY to fly.

"Let's go on a journey that will definitely make everyone go to sleep," said Fairy Grandmother. "We will all go - you [name] and Misti and me and the three sleepy teddy bear sisters. It's past their bed-time and they are very tired. They want to fall asleep now. Their names are Wynken, Blynken and Nod."

She picked up the little teddy bear girls and put them on the bed. They curled up close together, looking very weary. They could hardly keep their eyes open.

"Good night Misti and [name]," said Wynken slowly and drowsily.

"Sleep well Misti and [name]," said Blynken rubbing her eyes.

Tiny Nod just yawned [yawn] and snuggled down at the foot of the bed between her two sisters, too sleepy to say anything. She made little snoring noises as she slowly breathed in and out.

Fairy Grandmother stood behind the bed and waved her wand again.

Gradually your bedroom fades away and you, [name] find yourself lying in your own lovely, comfy bed next to Misti, in a magical place. You are at the top of a wide staircase, surrounded by beautiful autumn trees and stars.

You hear the sleepy sighing of the night breeze. It sounds like a gentle breath as it softly rustles through the leaves. The leaves are falling, falling down, down, showering down to the ground. The trees are swaying and nodding, the way your head nods when you are very <u>sleepy</u>.

This is a safe, comfortable place, and you are snug in your very own bed.

Fairy Grandmother says, "Misti and [name], your home is at the bottom of the magic staircase. We are going to float slowly and peacefully down the magic staircase in the bed. Along the way we will meet our friends the Drowsy Puppy and Snuggles the Squirrel. They will help us to fall asleep easily.

"When we reach your own home down there at the bottom of the staircase I think you will certainly be asleep, but you might fall asleep before that."

Tiny teddy-bear Nod is already fast asleep now. Wynken and Blynken are almost asleep. They can hardly keep their heavy eyes open. Their heads are bent down on their chests and they are breathing slowly and deeply.

Everyone on and in the bed is safe and comfortable. Your sleepy friends will stay with you till morning, [name]. Even if you can't see them they will be there sleeping, snoring, breathing in breathing out, <u>breathing slowly</u> as they sleep deeply and peacefully and calmly.

The comfortable bed starts floating down, down and down. Down the wide stairs it floats, as the leaves softly fall down all around; falling deeper into relaxation as you are sinking deeper into the mattress of the comfortable bed.

After a while the bed gently stops beside a lovely puppy who is dozing on a soft, velvet bed with deep, cosy cushions.

The Drowsy Puppy is so tired she can only manage to open one eye.

"Hello Misti, hello [name]. Where are you going so slowly, drifting so peacefully?" she asks.

Misti says, "Hello Drowsy Puppy. We are floating down the sleepy staircase to [name's] own home, where we will fall fast asleep. Can you help us?"

"I find it easy to fall asleep," says the Drowsy Puppy. "Just breathe in and out slowly and deeply."

Then the Drowsy Puppy tells you a rhyme about slow, deep breathing.

"Take a deep breath, feel it fill you with calm.

Deep breathing works like a magical charm!

Slowly breathe in at the end of the day,

Slowly breathe out to send worries away.

Calm, soothing air fills your tummy and chest.

Deep breathing helps you to sink into rest,

Rising and falling like waves on the sea,

Gently and slowly, as calm as can be.

Peacefully breathing, air in and air out

Now you are sleepy, I'm sure there's no doubt."

"The more you and Misti breathe slowly," says the Drowsy Puppy, "the sleepier you both become. You become more tired and more relaxed. You sink down, down deeper into tiredness.

"You will remember about the breathing, Misti and [name], and tomorrow when you go to bed you will fall asleep even easier and quicker than now."

She yawns [yawn] and adds, "I think I might even fall asleep now… Good night!"

And she falls asleep easily on her soft, velvety bed.

Fairy Grandmother smiles sleepily, and very gently the bed starts floating down the staircase again. The slowly rocking bed is lightly falling down like a leaf from a tree. The softly rustling leaves are falling down all around; you are sinking <u>deeper,</u> becoming more and more <u>comfortable and lazy and tired</u>.

You have let go of all your thoughts and you are just breathing in and out, peacefully and calmly. At the foot of the bed two of the teddy bears are fast asleep and the last one, Wynken, is almost asleep now.

Slowly the bed glides to a stop underneath an over-hanging branch. On the branch lies a dozy squirrel who is half-asleep.

"Hello Misti and [name]," the squirrel says, yawning [yawn].

"Hello Snuggles," says Misti. She only murmurs softly, because she is so sleepy. "Can you help us go to sleep now?" She is too tired to say anything more.

"I have a good plan for falling asleep," says Snuggles. "Do you know how to tense up your muscles?"

Misti nods her head sleepily.

"Here's the plan," says Snuggles. "Starting with your feet you are going to tense them as tightly as you can, then let go and relax them completely. You are going to work your way from your feet to the top of your head.

"Now <u>breathe in</u> and think of your toes. Clench them really tightly. Then <u>breathe out</u> and let all the tightness flow out!"

Snuggles tells everyone a rhyme about relaxing, and while you are listening to it, [name], you are relaxing your muscles too.

"Curl your toes downward. Keep squeezing them tight,

Then let them go. They will feel soft and light!

Pull your toes upward to tighten your calves.

Let them <u>relax</u> - we don't do things by halves!

"Clench up your thighs just as hard as you can.

Now let them <u>rest,</u> like I said in the plan.

Clench your fists next, till they're tight as a stone.

Open your hands now. How limp they have grown!

"Make fists again, and curl up each strong arm.

Feel your tense muscles, then feel them go <u>calm.</u>

Suck in your tummy until it feels hollow,

Then let it loose. <u>Relaxation</u> will follow!

"Tighten your back - yes it feels rather good.

Then set it <u>free to relax</u> as it should.

Take a <u>deep breath</u> now and tighten your chest

Next breathe out <u>slowly</u> and <u>have a good rest.</u>

"Shrug up your shoulders, then let them release.

Soon you'll be sleeping in comfort and peace.

Screw up your face in a funny expression.

Now <u>smooth it out.</u> It's the end of our lesson!

"Heavily into your mattress you're sinking,

Comfy and <u>yawning</u>, too weary for thinking.

"You are good at relaxing, Misti and [name]," says Snuggles. "Tomorrow when you go to bed you will fall asleep even <u>easier and quicker</u> than now. Good night!"

Lying cuddled up beside you, [name], Misti is almost asleep. At the foot of the bed Wynken the teddy bear is fast asleep with her two sisters.

The bed with all its drowsy passengers safely floats down the stairs again, while rocking gently. Soon it reaches the bottom of the staircase.

Everyone is back in [name's] room again. Fairy Grandmother sits on a comfy magic armchair beside the bed. Her head is nodding and she looks very tired, as if she could fall asleep easily, any time.

"Mist and [name]", she says, "before I left Sleepyland I filled my pockets with magic petals from the sweet-dream flowers. They smell nice, and their magic is so powerful that when I say a magic rhyme and sprinkle them over you, they always make you fall asleep straight away. And tomorrow you will fall asleep even more quickly and easily!"
Misti is too sleepy to reply.

Fairy Grandmother reaches into the pockets of her pretty dress. She brings out handfuls of sweet-smelling petals, pink and blue and yellow, and sprinkles them over your bed [mimic the sprinkling action].

<u>Slowly and peacefully</u> she says the magic spell:

"More and more <u>weary</u> with each breath you take,
Harder and harder to stay quite awake.
Heavy so heavy your eyelids must close,
<u>Sleepy so sleepy</u> you're longing to doze.

"Countdown from three, down to two, then to one.
One means your calm, peaceful sleep has begun.
Three, two, one, sleep. You just <u>let go</u> and sink.
Fall into sleep without having to think.

Every night you will fall asleep better.
Open eyes, closed eyes — it just doesn't matter.
Even with open eyes you're just <u>too weary.</u>
Maybe you'll close them before they get bleary.
Sleepy now, sleepy now, sink into bed.
Peaceful and weary now, lay down your head.
Closing your eyes you let go of the day,
Yawning and yawning now; drifting away."

Now even Fairy Grandmother is asleep, comfortable in her arm chair. You can see that everyone is asleep, so you close your eyes and go to sleep too.

About the author and the book

I have written several children's stories, some of which are in rhyme. I am also the mother of three daughters.

Upon reading Carl-Johan Forssén Ehrlin's "The Rabbit Who Wants To Fall Asleep" I was impressed by the concept of using a storybook to help children go to sleep.

When I was a little girl I would have liked to hear a story about a little creature who was more like me, and I'm sure that when my daughters were very young they would have liked that too. That is why I decided to write a 'go to sleep story' about a girl-kitten.

The story is not, however, intended solely for girls. Just as girls enjoy the story of Roger the Rabbit, so boys can enjoy the tale of Misti the Kitten.

Psychological Sleep Techniques

Like most people I occasionally have difficulty getting to sleep. To help with this problem I learned common psychological sleep induction techniques such as —

- putting aside troublesome thoughts until the following day (as an adult, this is generally achieved by writing them down on paper)
- breathing deeply
- slowing down
- visualizing a safe and peaceful place
- imagining a descent, including the sensations of sinking and heaviness
- progressive muscle relaxation
- using sleep-triggering words
- employing the 'infectiousness' of yawning

One particular sequence for sleep techniques is most effective. The first thing to do is reassure your audience that what you are about to say to them will have a powerful effect; that you can, in fact, use words to make them go to sleep. You also reassure them that they are in a a place that is safe to sleep, where they can let go and relax because they do not have to be vigilant.

Give them permission to fall asleep before the story ends, so that they don't feel obliged to stay awake and they won't feel they've let you down by nodding off.

Next, you ask them to visualize doing things that make them tired, such as physical activities.

Create a sense of descent; ask them to imagine a safe, gentle downward motion.

Introduce the concept of deep breathing, (also called abdominal breathing). Many cultures across the world use deep breathing to reduce anxiety and stress, and promote a sense of tranquillity.

Deep breathing increases the brain's oxygen supply, thereby stimulating the parasympathetic nervous system. This slows the heart rate and brings about a state of calmness. Slow, deep breathing helps quieten your thoughts and helps you feel connected to your body.

Progressive muscle relaxation comes next, combined with imagery suggesting heaviness of the body, especially the eyelids.

A kind of 'placebo' effect can be a powerful tool in sleep induction. With this technique you describe a potent magical spell or potion or action that will 'definitely' bring on sleep.

Visualizing other people peacefully asleep nearby is also a strong sleep signal.

Conclude your sleep induction sequence with evening customs and traditions that signal sleep-time, such as a kiss on the cheek or forehead, tucking in the blankets and saying 'good night'.

Such sleep induction techniques are well-known, and indeed if you Google 'psychological sleep techniques' you will find them all over the Internet.

Hypnotic Poems

Additionally, in "The Kitten Who Wants To Fall Asleep" the hypnotic power of rhyme and rhythm has been used to help make the story more effective.

Some people feel worried when they hear the term 'hypnotic'. They may be unaware that all hypnosis is completely voluntary. Hypnosis is not a form of mind control — it does not turn people into zombies! It merely helps us to focus our attention, of our own free will.

Besides, simply hearing a simple child's poem with a calming, hypnotic rhythm is quite different from undergoing professional hypnotherapy.

Hypnotic induction techniques are similar to sleep induction techniques. Both are used to promote deep relaxation. Sometimes relaxation methods take the form of hypnotic poems. Songs and lullabies have traditionally been used to lull children to sleep. Hypnotic induction poetry works the same way.

The poems in 'The Kitten Who Wants To Fall Asleep' are in 3/4 time, better known as 'waltz time'. It is a relaxing, lulling rhythm resembling the swaying motion of a mother rocking a cradle or a father walking back and forth with a baby in his arms, calming an infant. Every parent knows that gentle rocking rhythms can soothe a child. Some of the best known lullabies have the 3/4 time signature, including —

"Rockabye Baby"
"Brahms' Lullaby"
"Lavender's Blue"
"Good Night", by the Beatles.

In calming poems, the rhyming is as important as the rhythm.

Blogger Ken Myers wrote, "The placement of rhyming words and the establishment of structure, meter and vocal rhythm in a poem can significantly affect the way it sounds when read aloud. Fans of the formal rhyming styles insist that rhymes are necessary in terms of establishing rhythm.

"Kids are wild about poems that rhyme... From helping kids remember the words to their favorite verses to making it fun for them to recite, rhyming words are a cornerstone of kids' poetry."[1]

Acknowledgement

Carl-Johan Forssén Ehrlin's work is the inspiration for this book, and I am indebted to him for his useful idea of weaving tried-and-true sleep induction methods into a children's bedtime story.

Cecilia Egan

---

1   "10 Reasons Every Poem Should Rhyme and How it Could Impact You Big Time" by Kenney Myers. Published on 04/03/2013. www.kenneymyers.com

Other books in the series 'The Kitten Who ...'

The Kitten Who Wants to Say Goodbye to Diapers:
A Story to Help Children Use The Potty

What is different about this children's toilet-training book?

It uses language patterns and proven, powerful psychological techniques that really get results.

Motivation is the key to toilet training. This story is designed to be gently persuasive on both the conscious and unconscious levels.

It should be be read aloud to children by an older person, and is intended as an aid to any potty-training method.

The psychological methods woven into this tale will make training quicker and easier. Simple rhyming verses add an extra element of fun.

Many concepts are common to all potty-training methods. They are based on motivations that are natural in all healthy children.

These include:
- Imitation – seeing a person or a 'drink and wet' doll using a toilet or potty and wanting to copy.
- Wanting to be independent and feel like a grown-up
- Peer pressure – seeing siblings or other toddlers successfully using the potty
- Wanting to be praiseworthy
- Wanting to feel dry
- Wanting to feel clean

To help children learn, the story is interactive. You can read out questions for the child to answer, and you can ask the child to point to images on the pages.

Parents, relax! Just read the story to your little ones and enjoy helping them learn to master this important skill.

Other books in the series 'The Kitten Who ...'

The Kitten Who Wants to be the Boss of her Temper:
A Story to Help Children Deal with Tantrums

What if you could read your children a story incorporating effective psychological methods to help them learn to manage anger?

Many parents worry about young children behaving aggressively when they feel upset. Much of this is normal for youngsters. Nevertheless, these issues do need to be addressed.

Psychological anger management techniques include:
- 'Breathing out' the anger with slow, deep breaths.
- Counting to ten slowly, to give angry feelings some time to subside.
- Moving away from the problem situation until you feel calmer.
- Squeezing or pummelling a soft, inanimate object such as a cushion, which cannot be hurt and which cannot hurt you.
- Engaging in vigorous physical activities such as running, cycling, dancing or even housework, as an outlet for pent-up feelings.
- Lying down and listening to relaxing music, or sleeping.
- When you feel calmer, talking about your feelings with someone you trust.

This story also harnesses the mnemonic power of visual association and simple rhyming verse to make learning fun and the techniques easier to remember.

Just as children respond to Cecilia Egan's sleep-inducing story 'The Kitten Who Wants to Fall Asleep," so they can learn to be the boss of their temper while listening to this tale.

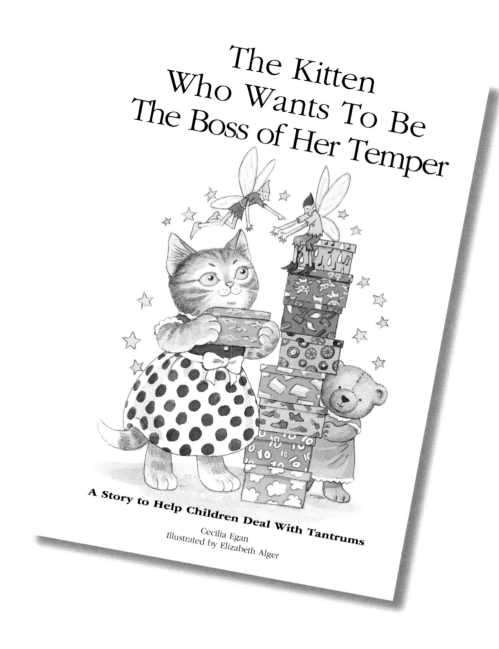

The Kitten Who Wants To Be The Boss of Her Temper

A Story to Help Children Deal With Tantrums

Cecilia Egan
Illustrated by Elizabeth Alger

Made in the USA
San Bernardino, CA
08 August 2017